Magic
Animal Friends

For Ruby Harris-Lenthall
With Love

Special thanks to Valerie Wilding

ORCHARD BOOKS

First published in Great Britain in 2016 by The Watts Publishing Group

1 3 5 7 9 10 8 6 4 2

Text © Working Partners Ltd 2016
Illustrations © Orchard Books 2016

A CIP catalogue record for this book is available from the British Library.

ISBN 978 1 40834 108 7

Printed in Great Britain

The paper and board used in this book are made from wood from responsible sources

Orchard Books
An imprint of Hachette Children's Group
Part of The Watts Publishing Group Limited
Carmelite House, 50 Victoria Embankment, London EC4Y 0DZ

An Hachette UK Company
www.hachette.co.uk
www.hachettechildrens.co.uk

Freya Snufflenose's Lost Laugh

Daisy Meadows

ORCHARD

Map of Friendship Forest

Woollyhop Shop

Harmony Hall Theatre

Petal Hill

Garland Green

Cherry Tree Corner

Treasure Tree

Bluebell Brook

Agatha Glitterwing's Shop

Slipperslide's Home

Sparklepaw Cottage

Coral Cove

Grizelda's Tower

Witchy Waste

Summer Sands Beach

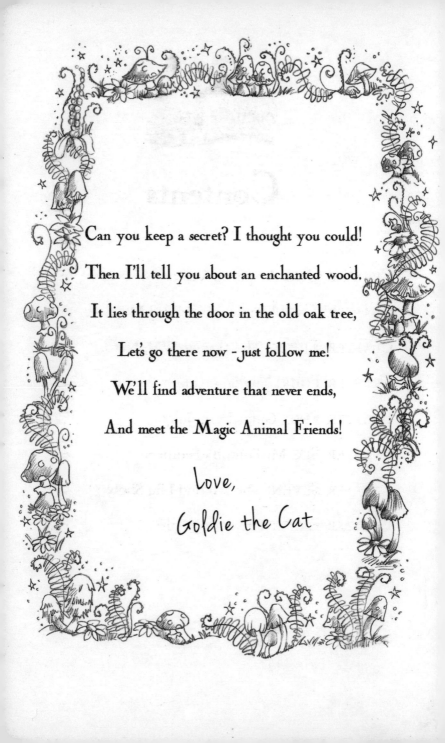

Can you keep a secret? I thought you could!

Then I'll tell you about an enchanted wood.

It lies through the door in the old oak tree,

Let's go there now - just follow me!

We'll find adventure that never ends,

And meet the Magic Animal Friends!

Love,
Goldie the Cat

Contents

CHAPTER ONE

A Special Visitor

"Look!" Lily Hart said to her best friend, Jess Forester. "They're playing with our little toys!"

A bunny with a sore ear and a guinea pig with his leg in a tiny splint were in an animal pen, playing with a ball the girls had made from Mr Forester's old gloves.

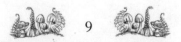

They were two of the animal patients at the Helping Paw Wildlife Hospital, which was run by Lily's parents in a barn in their garden.

"They are so sweet!" Jess said.

Lily and Jess were sitting on a rug in the Harts' garden, threading cotton reels together. Beside them was a bag full of string, cardboard tubes and old clothes.

Lily held up an old pair of jeans. "If we cut off the legs and stuff them with straw, they'll make great tug-of-war toys!"

"Good idea!" said Jess. Then she took a long ribbon with bells hanging from

it and dangled it in the air. Three snowy
white kittens, who were getting over bad
colds, raced over to
jump up and pat
the jingling bells.

In a pen close by,
a fox cub sat with
his ears drooped.

"All of the
other animals
love playing
with the toys
we've made,"
said Jess.

"I wonder why he doesn't want to play?"

"I don't know," said Lily. "Perhaps we just haven't found the right toy yet…" She stopped, and grinned in delight as a golden cat bounded across the grass towards them. "Goldie!" she cried.

The beautiful green-eyed cat rubbed against their legs, mewing softly.

The girls were thrilled to see her. Goldie was their special friend, and she lived in a secret place called Friendship Forest. It was

 12

a magical world where the animals lived in pretty little cottages and dens, and all of them could talk!

Jess's eyes shone. "Goldie must have come to take us back to Friendship Forest," she said. "Maybe we'll have another adventure!"

"I hope so!" cried Lily. Then she frowned. "I just hope Grizelda isn't causing trouble again," she said.

Grizelda was a horrible witch who wanted to drive all the animals out of Friendship Forest so she could have it all for herself. Goldie and the girls had

managed to stop her so far, but they knew
that Grizelda wouldn't give up.

Goldie ran towards Brightley Stream
at the bottom of the garden. Lily and Jess
raced after Goldie, across the stepping
stones and into Brightley Meadow.
Since no time passed while they were in
Friendship Forest, they knew that all their
things would be waiting for them when
they got back.

Goldie led the girls to a lifeless old
oak tree in the middle of the meadow.
As soon as she reached it, new leaves,
as green as her eyes, sprang from every

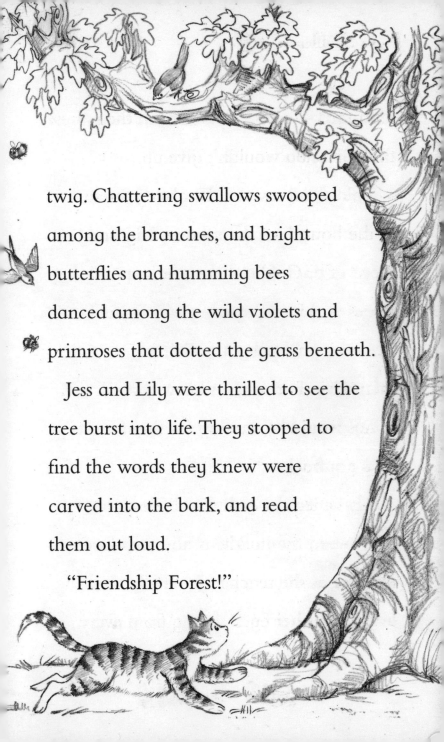

twig. Chattering swallows swooped among the branches, and bright butterflies and humming bees danced among the wild violets and primroses that dotted the grass beneath.

Jess and Lily were thrilled to see the tree burst into life. They stooped to find the words they knew were carved into the bark, and read them out loud.

"Friendship Forest!"

Instantly, a door appeared in the trunk and Goldie bounded inside.

The girls exchanged excited glances and followed her into the shimmering glow. A tingle ran through them and they knew they were growing a little smaller.

As the golden light faded, they found themselves in a sunlit forest glade.

"Welcome back to Friendship Forest," said a soft voice.

Lily turned. "Goldie!"

The beautiful cat was now standing upright, as tall as their shoulders, wearing her golden scarf.

"You can talk to us at last!" said Jess.

The three friends hugged.

Jess was worried. "Is Grizelda causing trouble again?"

Goldie shook her head. "Ever since we broke the spell she put on the Memory Tree, no one has seen her," she said.

The Memory Tree was one of four Heart Trees in Friendship Forest. The others were the Laughter Tree, the Sweet Dreams Tree and the Kindness Tree, and the animals relied on them whenever they needed a good giggle, a restful sleep or a helping hand.

Grizelda and Thistle, her young apprentice witch, had already tried to ruin the Memory Tree's magic by breaking its heart into three pieces, but Goldie and the girls had found them again and saved the tree.

Once Thistle had discovered what a wonderful place the forest was, she had stayed to guard the Memory Tree. But horrid Grizelda still had three more apprentice witches to help her cause trouble – Nettle, Dandelion and Ivy.

"I bet Grizelda will soon make a new plan to attack the rest of the Heart Trees," said Lily.

Goldie nodded. "I know," she said, "but that's not why I've brought you here. This afternoon it's the Funny Fair in Merry Meadow. You must come and watch. It's hilarious!"

She took a hand in each paw and they set off through the forest along a mossy path lined with sunberry bushes full of golden berries.

As they climbed a low hill, Jess stopped.

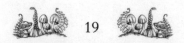

"Listen!" she said.

They heard chattering voices and laughter up ahead.

Goldie smiled. "We're almost at Merry Meadow."

At the top of the hill, they pushed through tall curling ferns and looked down into a wide grassy clearing. Animals were everywhere, all of them wearing brightly coloured costumes. Some were dancing, some were doing tricks – and all of them were laughing!

Lily grinned at Jess. "This is going to be so much fun!"

CHAPTER TWO

Laughter in Merry Meadow

"The animals are practising for the Funny

Fair," Goldie explained.

Lily pointed to a puppy riding a

unicycle. "There's Patch Muddlepup!"

He spotted her and waved.

"And the Twinkletails!" said Jess,

pointing out a row of mice. They were
wearing red noses and had curled their
whiskers. "They look funny!"

Lily burst out laughing. "Look at
Amelia Sparklepaw's juggling!" she cried.

The little white kitten was wearing a
bouncy red polka-dotted skirt and big
brown boots. She was juggling walnuts,
until one by one she made them come
down – *plonk!* – right on top of her head.

There were shrieks of laughter.

"Hello, down there!" cried a voice
above them. They looked up to see
Mr Cleverfeather the owl swinging an

enormous shimmering silver net
in the air. It was half-filled with
pink and yellow swirls.
"Welcome back,
Jiss and Lelly," he said,
getting his words muddled
up as usual. "This is my
Laugh Catcher. I've
invented a machine called
the Joke-o-matic and I need to
catch enough laughter to power it."

Mr Cleverfeather pointed a wing to
where a big orange funnel was lying on
its side. At the narrow end of the funnel

was a big empty sack.

"What does the Joke-o-matic do?" asked Jess.

"It jells tunny fokes, of course," said Mr Cleverfeather. "I mean—"

Everyone giggled.

"You mean it tells funny jokes," explained Goldie.

The owl beamed. "Exactly! But first I have to fill that sack with laughter."

Jess nudged Lily. "Look at that adorable little dormouse doing acrobatics," she said.

The tiny golden-brown creature had soft round ears, delicate whiskers and a long fluffy tail. She finished with three roly-polys, then sprang to her feet. As everyone clapped, she picked up her blue handbag and a large purple flower, which she tucked behind her ear.

Jess knelt beside her. "Hello!" she said. "I'm Jess, and this is my best friend, Lily."

The dormouse's big dark eyes sparkled.

"I'm Freya Snufflenose!" she told them.

"I like your purple flower," said Jess.

Freya giggled. "Would you like to smell it?" she asked.

As Jess leaned over to sniff the flower, it puffed a cloud of silver glitter all over the dormouse's soft fur.

"Oh, no!" Freya cried. "My joke glitter flower was supposed to puff all over Jess. Bother!" she said sadly. "I just keep getting it wrong."

"The glitter looks pretty on your fur," said Lily.

"Thanks!" said Freya. "I love telling jokes too, but sometimes I get nervous in front of an audience."

"Why don't you tell us one now?" Jess suggested.

Freya took a deep breath. "OK, here goes," she said. "A donkey walked into the Toadstool Café and said—" She stopped. "Bother! I got it wrong."

She tried again. "What happened when a wonkey walked—? Bother! Bother! Wrong again! See?" The little dormouse

looked at her paws sadly. "I always forget
how to tell the joke."

"Don't worry," said Lily. "I'm sure
you'll get it right soon!" She put her hand
down and Freya jumped onto it. She was
so small she fitted neatly into Lily's palm.

Freya looked up at the girls. Her wide
dark eyes swam with tears. "I love making
everyone laugh," she said, "and I'm
supposed to be telling jokes at the show
later, but I just don't know if I can do it in
front of all my friends!"

Jess turned to Goldie. "One of the Heart
Trees is called the Laughter Tree, isn't it?"

she asked. "Do you think it would help if we took Freya there?"

"Of course!" said Goldie. "That's where all the animals go when they need cheering up."

"Let's try it," Lily said. She gently stroked the little dormouse as a big tear dropped onto the palm of her hand.

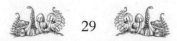

Lily bent her head and whispered to the dormouse, "Perhaps you could practise your jokes there?"

Freya's ears perked up. "Yes, please!" she said. "If anything in Friendship Forest can help me make people laugh, it's the Laughter Tree!"

CHAPTER THREE

The Trouble With Nettle

Lily popped Freya on her shoulder and followed Jess and Goldie through the forest. The dormouse curled her fluffy tail around Lily's ear.

"I'm just making sure I don't fall off," she said. As they started walking, Freya

 31

began whistling a little squeaky song that made the girls giggle.

"Even your songs are funny!" Lily said with a laugh.

"Here's the Heart Path," Goldie called over her shoulder.

The mossy path followed a heart shape, and it linked all four Heart Trees. The part they were on was lined with sunny yellow flowers that had glossy, deep green leaves. They smelled like delicious lemon drops.

Before long, the friends reached a small clearing

with a tall tree in the middle. Its delicate
branches hung down towards the grass.

"The Laughter Tree!" said Goldie.

"It's so beautiful!" said Jess.

The tree's long feathery leaves wafted
in the breeze, while butterflies fluttered
and bees buzzed happily among its tiny
white flowers.

The dormouse's jolly song faded away
as she caught sight of the tree. "Oh,
wow!" she cried.

"Look there!" cried Jess,
pointing to a hollow in the
middle of the trunk.

A glowing golden heart nestled inside,
sparkling merrily. Just like all the other
Heart Trees, the heart was the source
of the tree's special magic, giving it the
power to cheer up anyone in the forest
who came to visit.

Freya clapped her paws in delight, and Lily lowered her to the ground. The little dormouse scampered to the tree. "I feel happier already!" she cried, looking up at it. "Listen! The butterflies and bees are giggling, too!"

The girls listened – and grinned when they heard the very faint, tinkling laughter.

"I feel happier, too," said Lily.

"And me," said Jess, "even though I wasn't sad before!"

"It's the Laughter Tree's magic," said Goldie with a smile.

Lily and Jess walked closer to the

tree, and were

surprised

when the

feathery

branches

reached out

to tickle them.

The girls broke

into peals of

laughter as the branches wiggled all

around their sides.

Freya ran up to the tree, and another

branch reached out to tickle her all over

too. She couldn't stop laughing! "This is so funny," she said with a giggle. "Especially when it tickles my ears!"

But Jess had spotted something. "Oh, no!" she said, pointing to the edge of the clearing.

Two orbs, one smaller than the other, floated towards them.

"It's Grizelda and one of her witch helpers!" Goldie cried in alarm.

Lily scooped Freya up and huddled with Jess and Goldie. For a moment, the only sound was the tinkling giggles of insects, high in the tree.

The larger orb burst in a shower of smelly sparks. In its place stood a tall witch wearing a purple tunic over skinny black trousers and high, pointy boots. Her green hair writhed around her head as if it was alive.

"Grizelda!" Jess cried.

The witch cackled. "Not just me!" she said. "I've brought Nettle, too!" The smaller orb burst into sparks, and a young witch with spiky green hair and folded arms appeared.

"Boo!" said Nettle.

Lily folded her arms, too. "You don't

38

scare us, Nettle," she said firmly.

The apprentice witch stamped her foot and said crossly, "Humpity grumpity!"

"What are you up to now, Grizelda?" Jess asked fiercely.

The witch cackled again. "I've got a

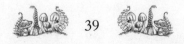

new plan to drive all the silly animals out of Friendship Forest — for good!"

"We'll stop you!" cried Lily.

The witch shrieked with laughter. "You won't! When I ruin the Laughter Tree's heart, everyone will be miserable. The only way to escape the misery will be to leave the forest! Ha haa!"

She pointed a bony finger towards the Laughter Tree.

"No!" Jess dived to protect the heart.

She was too late. Sparks from Grizelda's

finger shot into the hollow and struck the heart with a terrible crack.

The heart's glow blazed for a moment, then faded away. It turned grey and dull. All of a sudden, all the happy sounds of the forest seemed to go quiet.

The butterflies and bees fell silent. The leaves drooped and were still.

As Jess, Lily, Goldie and Freya stared in dismay, Grizelda cackled. "Nettle will make sure you never fix that heart!"

The apprentice witch scowled at the four friends.

Grizelda raised a hand. "Nothing can stop my plan," she jeered. With a snap of her fingers, she disappeared in a shower of stinking sparks.

As the girls stared after the witch, Nettle jumped at them, yelling, "Yaaaaah!"

Jess turned to her. "That's not scary, Nettle! Go away!"

"Humpity grumpity!" Nettle scowled. "I'll get you yet! Don't even try to fix the heart – because I'll stop you!" Then she, too, snapped her fingers and vanished.

Freya, who had been falling over with laughter just moments before the witches arrived, had gone quiet. She clutched her handbag. "It won't be Friendship Forest without happiness and laughter," she whimpered. "Can't we do something?"

"Poor Freya," Jess said. "She's lost her laugh, just like the rest of the forest."

43

Goldie tickled Freya's ears. "Cheer up," she said. "The girls will do their best to make the heart better."

"Of course we will," said Lily, though she didn't know how.

But Jess had been thinking. "I've got an idea," she said. "We need Great-Uncle Greybear!"

CHAPTER FOUR

The Sad Café

"Of course!" said Lily. "Great-Uncle Greybear can help us."

Great-Uncle Greybear was the oldest animal in the forest. The girls had used his old scrapbook to fix the first Heart Tree that Grizelda had broken.

"The scrapbook told us the secret to

fixing the Memory Tree the last time we were here," said Jess. "Maybe it can tell us how to fix the Laughter Tree too!"

"Brilliant!" said Goldie.

Freya dabbed her tears with a tiny blue hanky from her bag. "Where is Great-Uncle Greybear?"

"He was in the Toadstool Café when I passed this morning," said Goldie. "Maybe he's still there."

"Let's hurry," said Lily. "It'll be lovely to see some of our friends at the café. It's always such a happy place!"

She tucked Freya into her pocket and

46

off they went. They leapt over logs and rocks and skidded around bushes as they raced through the forest.

As usual, there were lots of animals in Toadstool Glade, and the café was busy. All the outside tables were full.

"Hello!" Jess and Lily called, waving to their friends. But no one smiled or waved back. There was none of the usual chatter and laughter. Ruby Fuzzybrush the fox and Lottie Littlestripe the badger were sitting silently, and the Tabbypaw cat family huddled miserably together.

Everyone looked sad.

47

"Oh, no," groaned Jess. "Without the magic of the Laughter Tree, everyone is so gloomy!"

Freya's eyes went wide. "Does that mean we'll be sad, too?" she asked. "I don't want to be sad."

Lily patted Freya on her furry head. "Don't worry, Freya," she said. "Jess and I aren't affected because we're from the human world. If you start feeling sad, we'll cheer you up straight away!"

"Thanks!" Freya said. "And if you start getting sad, I'll cheer you up as well!"

They all grinned. "Come on," said

Goldie, "let's find Great-Uncle Greybear."

They went to the café tables. Mr Cleverfeather was sitting at one, frowning at his drink. "Hello, Jilly and Less," he said glumly. "And Foldie and Greya. I got a cup of my favourite hazelnut whirl tea, but I feel too sad to drink it."

The owl looked so glum that the girls didn't feel like giggling when he muddled his words. "He was so happy when we saw him at Merry Meadow," Lily whispered to Jess. "This is awful!"

Mr Longwhiskers the rabbit came over, wearing his usual waiter's apron. "Hello," he said. "Miserable day, isn't it?"

Jess looked at Lily, dismayed. "Everyone in the whole glade is sad!" she said.

Lily spotted a big bear sitting near the café door, his walking stick propped up against his chair. He was staring down at the bowl in front of him. "There's Great-Uncle Greybear!" she said.

The grey bear looked up and gave a great big gruffly sigh.

"Hello," he said. "Usually I love my chestnut porridge with honey, but not today." He pushed the bowl away and sighed once more. "I wish I could feel happy again."

Freya jumped off Lily's shoulder, onto the table, and looked up at him. "You will," she said, "but we need your help to bring laughter back to Friendship Forest."

Great-Uncle Greybear ruffled Freya's fur with his

great big paw. "Me? How could I help?"
he asked.

"We need to borrow your scrapbook
again," said Freya.

"Would you lend it to us?" Jess asked.

Great-Uncle Greybear nodded. "I've got
my scrapbook right here in my basket!"
he said. "I was taking it to the library to
ask Mrs Taptree the woodpecker to put a
new cover on it. Something cheerful, I was
thinking, but it doesn't matter now…"

Lily put her arm round his big shoulders.
"Of course it does. We'll cheer you up," she
promised. "And all the other animals too."

Great-Uncle Greybear handed them the scrapbook and they gathered around.

When Goldie turned the last page, Freya gave a squeak.

"Look!" she cried. "It says, 'A Potion to Fill a Heart with Laughter.'"

"Clever Freya!" said Jess. She read the recipe out loud.

"*Take giggleberry juice, and a feather that's loose, (but it must be the tickliest ever!)*

To cheer up the heart, here's the hardest part,

So you'll have to be doubly clever.

Catch a laugh that's the first ever to burst,

From someone who's never laughed – never!

Mix it all in a dish. Pour it out with a wish,

And the heart will be happy forever."

"It doesn't say that the potion is for the heart of a Heart Tree, though," Jess said. "Do you think it will work?"

"It's the best plan we've got," said Lily. Everyone agreed.

"OK," Lily continued. "So we need giggleberry juice, the tickliest feather in the forest, and someone's first-ever laugh."

Goldie grinned. "The café serves giggleberry pies!"

Jess called to Mrs Longwhiskers. "May we have some giggleberries?"

The rabbit gave a sad sigh. "You can get some from the giggleberry bush," she said, pointing to a bush with bright red leaves growing beneath the café window. "But if you pick the berries, they'll shrivel up. The only way to get giggleberries is to make the bush giggle. And I don't know how to do that any more."

Jess grinned. "I bet Freya does," she said. "She loves making the animals laugh. I bet she can make the bush giggle, too!"

CHAPTER FIVE

Giggleberry Juice

Freya Snufflenose hopped down from
the table and scampered over to the
giggleberry bush. Hanging among
the red leaves were bunches of bright
purple giggleberries. "I've never made
a plant laugh before!" she said, sniffing
the berries.

Mrs Longwhiskers placed a yellow dish with a lid beside Freya. "You'll need this to catch the berries," she said.

Jess, Lily and Goldie knelt beside Freya. "You can do it," said Jess. "You're a very funny dormouse."

"Here goes!" said Freya. The little dormouse made a funny face at the bush.

The leaves rustled.

"Try again," said Lily.

Freya turned a roly-poly, then bounced along on her bottom.

A tiny giggling sound came from the bush. A moment later, the bush dropped

one of its berries on the ground. Jess

picked it up and squeezed its purple juice

into the yellow dish.

Freya did a silly hopping dance next,

which made Goldie and the girls laugh.

The giggling sound grew louder, and

down fell a whole clump of berries.

Goldie glanced around at the animals

sitting at the café tables. "The giggleberry

bush finds Freya funny," she whispered,

"but none of the animals are smiling. We must fix the Laughter Tree's heart soon."

The bush giggled as Freya pretended to trip over her furry tail.

More berries fell.

Jess squeezed another handful then said, "I think that's enough." She put the lid on.

Lily put her hand on the ground and Freya climbed into her palm.

"Whew! I'm tired now," she said.

"You can ride on my shoulder while we look for the feather," said Lily.

Freya snuggled into Lily's neck, and began whistling a new song. "I miss the

Laughter Tree," she said, pausing in the middle. "Its tickly branches reminded me of my mum's old feather duster. It was the tickliest thing ever!"

Jess glanced excitedly at Lily and Goldie. "It sounds like we need the same feathers!" she said. "Freya, do you know which bird they came from?"

"Mr Fantail the peacock," said Freya. "He makes feather dusters."

Goldie clapped her paws. "That's wonderful, Freya!" she said. "Mr Fantail lives on Hyacinth Hill. Maybe he'll give us one of his feathers. Let's go and see."

"We'd better keep our ears open too," said Lily, as they hurried past the café tables. "We still need to find a laugh from someone who's never laughed before."

"Then you'll theed niss!" cried Mr Cleverfeather, fluttering from his chair. He handed Jess his Laugh Catcher. "I mean, you'll need this." His feathers ruffled as he sighed. "No one's laughing here, so I can't use it."

Jess gave him a big hug. "Thank you, Mr Cleverfeather."

The friends raced through the trees until they reached Hyacinth Hill. They

made their way
upwards through
pink, blue and
mauve blooms.
"Isn't it pretty!"
Freya said,

jumping up and down on Lily's shoulder.

They soon reached a neat little
cottage, perched on a broad branch.
The glossy blue front door shone like a
jewel, and bright green curtains hung at
the windows. Neat window boxes were
filled with white daisies, and everything
sparkled in the sunlight.

They quickly climbed up to the house.
Goldie knocked on the door and a
handsome peacock appeared. He was
wearing an apron and had a spotlessly
clean dustpan tucked beneath his wing.
His long tail feathers were folded up, but
they shimmered with beautiful colours.

"Hello, Mr Fantail," said Goldie.

"We're sorry to interrupt your cleaning," said Lily, pointing to his dustpan.

The peacock looked at them curiously, his tail feathers rustling with every movement. "Quite all right, quite all right…but what can I do for you?"

"We want to cheer up everyone in the forest," said Freya, from her perch on Lily's shoulder. "Please may we have one of your beautiful tail feathers? It'll help us do a spell to put things back to normal."

Mr Fantail swept his long tail over the doorstep, just like a broom.

"I'm afraid I can't help you," he said. "I need all my feathers to keep my house clean. And, for some reason, I am feeling quite out of sorts today. So if you'll excuse me, I've got some more dusting to do."

As he began to close the door, Jess and Lily shared a worried glance. How would they get the tickliest feather now?

CHAPTER SIX

Mr Fantail's Feathers

Before Mr Fantail had closed the door, Freya clasped her paws together.

"Please, Mr Fantail," she said. Her dark eyes were wide. "We really, really need one of your feathers to help save Friendship Forest." She pointed to his tail. "Look, there's a loose one sticking out!"

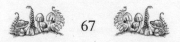

But Mr Fantail shook his head.

"So sorry, my dear, but I need all my
feathers to sweep the floors," he repeated.
"Wouldn't want to miss a spot!"

Freya buried her face in her tiny paws.
As she did so, she dropped her purple
glitter flower.

Jess caught it. But when her fingers
closed around the flower, it shot out a puff
of glitter.

Goldie and the girls gasped in horror
as silver sparkles sprayed all over the
peacock's tail.

"Oh, no!" Jess cried.

"We're sorry, Mr Fantail!" Lily said.
"We'll help you clean it up."

Mr Fantail stared at his glittery tail. At first, he looked shocked, then he started to smile. He spread his tail feathers so they stood upright in a shimmering fan.

"Oh, my!" he said. "Look how sparkly my feathers are! This is even better than having a squeaky-clean house!"

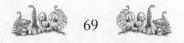

69

Lily and Jess grinned at each other.

"So maybe we could have your loose feather?" said Freya, looking hopeful.

"Of course, my friends!" Mr Fantail pulled it free and handed it to Lily. Then he removed a very short, bent feather. "And this one's rather untidy as well," he said, handing it to Jess.

"Thank you," she said.

"Bye, Mr Fantail!" they all called. They left the peacock admiring his glittering tail and climbed back down the tree.

When they were on the ground, Lily tickled Jess's neck with the feather.

Jess giggled. "That's even ticklier than the leaves on the Laughter Tree!"

"Hooray!" Freya cheered. "We've got two of the things we need."

"And we can get the last ingredient with this!" Lily added, pointing to Mr Cleverfeather's Laugh Catcher.

Jess frowned. "Yes, but we can't just catch any laugh. It has to be someone's very first laugh! How are we going to find one of those?"

"I know! Who's the youngest baby in the forest?" Lily asked.

"That's Carly Chatterbeak the cuckoo,"

Freya replied. "My mum babysits her sometimes. Mum says she chuckles and giggles all the time. Her first laugh was ages ago."

Goldie sighed. "The trouble is that Friendship Forest is usually such a happy place that everyone here has already laughed."

Lily looked around gloomily. "Then how will we ever break the spell?"

"We got the first two ingredients easily," Jess said, crossing her arms. "But it seems like the last ingredient is going to be the hardest one yet!"

Just then,
the leaves
above them
rustled.

Jess looked up just in time
to dodge a falling pine cone. "There's
someone up there!" she said.

Lily spotted a flash of spiky green hair
among the leaves.

"Nettle!" she cried.

The young witch jumped down.
"Scared you, didn't I?"

"No, you didn't!" said Lily. "Jess heard
you, and I saw your hair."

Nettle scowled. "Humpity grumpity!"

"You know, laughing is much more fun than scowling," said Jess.

Nettle scowled again. "I don't laugh. I never have. Laughing is silly."

Lily gasped. "Nettle's never

laughed!" she whispered to the others.

Jess's eyes shone. "Of course! We've never heard her cackling like the other witches. We've got to make her laugh, then we can catch it in Mr Cleverfeather's net!"

Lily turned to the witch. "Nettle," she said, "I bet we can make you laugh."

Nettle folded her arms and said grumpily, "No, you can't."

"We can," said Lily. "Freya's the funniest animal in the forest, so get ready to giggle!"

"You can do it, Freya," said Goldie.

But the little dormouse suddenly looked nervous. Her tail and her whiskers drooped. "I don't think I can," she said.

"I couldn't tell my jokes right before…"

Lily scooped up Freya and cuddled her. The dormouse gave a sad sigh.

"Don't worry, Freya," said Lily. "Jess and I will give it a try. Who knows, maybe we'll cheer up both of you at the same time!"

CHAPTER SEVEN

The Jess and Lily Show

Lily gently put Freya down on a wide toadstool.

"OK, here goes," said Lily. She turned to Nettle, put out her tongue, stuck her fingers in her ears and crossed her eyes.

The others giggled, but Nettle scowled.

"Here's a joke for you," said Jess. "What's orange and sounds like a parrot?"

Nettle shrugged.

"A carrot!" said Jess.

Goldie laughed and clapped her paws. Nettle rolled her eyes.

"This isn't working," muttered Lily.

Freya stood up on the toadstool. "I want to try," she said. "If you can tell jokes without being nervous, so can I!"

"That's great!" said Jess.

Freya took a deep breath. "Nettle," she called. "I've got a joke for you. What colour are hiccups?"

Nettle shrugged again.

"*Burp*le!" said Freya.

Goldie and the girls laughed and clapped, but Nettle's face was as scowly and grumpy as ever.

"Freya!" said Lily. "Your flower joke! Do it on me!"

The dormouse twitched her purple flower, and out puffed a cloud of glitter. It missed Lily completely, and showered all over Goldie's tail.

The cat leaped in the air with a surprised, "Meow!"

Nettle's mouth twitched, but it wasn't a proper smile. "That's silly!" she said, turning away.

"Wait!" cried Jess. She whispered to Freya, "Try your donkey joke again!"

The little dormouse began, "What happened in the café when…" Her voice trailed off. She tried again. "Um, did you see the donkey… Oh, bother!" The nervous look returned to Freya's face.

Nettle folded her arms and tapped her foot impatiently.

"You can do it, Freya!" Goldie said. "We know you can."

After a moment, Freya's face lit up. "I know!" she said. "Here's a brand-new joke. What's mean and horrible and bouncy?"

"We don't know," said the girls. "What is mean and horrible and bouncy?"

The little dormouse grinned. "Grizelda on a trampoline!"

Nettle's mouth twitched. Her eyes crinkled…

Jess and Lily held their breath.

Then Nettle gave a burst of laughter!

"Quick!" cried Lily.

Jess swished the Laugh Catcher over Nettle's head.

"I've got it!" she said, as a pink and yellow cloud appeared in the net, swirling around. "Hooray!"

Goldie quickly held out the dish with giggleberry juice inside and took off the lid. "Tip it into here!"

 82

Jess held the net over the dish and patted it until the pink and yellow swirl dropped into the giggleberry juice.

Lily used Mr Fantail's feather to swirl the mixture around. It bubbled and fizzed, turning bright yellow.

Jess drew a deep breath. "Well, we've made the potion – let's just hope it works on the Laughter Tree's broken heart! Come on, everyone. Let's go!"

They left Nettle behind them, rolling around on the ground, still shaking with uncontrollable giggles. Now that she'd started laughing, she couldn't stop!

Goldie carefully lifted the grey heart out of the hollow in the Laughter Tree's trunk.

Jess held the dish of potion over it.

"Wait!" said Freya. "The potion spell said, 'Pour it out with a wish.'"

"You're right," said Jess. "But what should we wish for?"

After a moment, Lily said, "I've thought of something. Ready?"

Jess nodded, and as she poured the potion over the heart, Lily said, "We wish for the tree to bring laughter to Friendship Forest for ever!"

A cloud of yellow sparkles surrounded the dull grey heart.

Lily squeezed Jess's hand. "It's working!"

As the sparkles cleared, the heart glowed golden. The leaves of the Laughter Tree rustled as they sprang back to life.

"Hooray!" cried Goldie.

Freya's eyes lit up. "I feel so happy!" She twirled around, giggling.

A laugh came from behind them.

"It's Nettle!" said Lily, dismayed. "She followed us."

Jess groaned. "Have you come to cause trouble?" she asked Nettle.

To their surprise, the young witch smiled. "Oh, no!" she said. "I just wanted to tell you that I was wrong about laughing being silly. Laughing is great!"

Jess grinned. "It is!"

Freya scampered on to a fallen log and hopped backwards all along it, turned a cartwheel off the end, then stuck her tongue out and waggled her ears.

Nettle squealed with laughter, giggling so much that her spiky green hair shook! The girls and Goldie joined in. Now that the Laughter Tree was fixed, everyone felt much, much happier.

Until they spied a yellow orb of light floating through the trees towards them!

"Look out!" cried Jess, scooping Freya into her arms.

The orb burst into stinky sparks and Grizelda appeared.

She looked furious. Her face was red with rage, and her hair stuck out from her head like stiff seaweed.

"Nettle!" she shrieked. "You've ruined my plan!"

Lily and Jess stood either side of Nettle.

"Don't be afraid," Lily whispered.

The young witch stepped forward. "I'm having fun," she said to Grizelda. "You should try it!"

"No!" Grizelda stamped her feet. "Stop grinning like that, Nettle!"

Nettle's grin became even wider. "Sorry, Grizelda," she said, "but I'm not going to help you with your horrible spells any more. I like laughing and I like Friendship Forest. I'm staying here with my friends."

She looked around at Goldie, Freya and the girls. "That is, if they want me to."

88

They all nodded. "Yes, we do!"

"Oh, dear," whispered Freya. "Grizelda's
so cross her face looks like an angry
tomato!"

The three friends and Nettle couldn't
help laughing again.

"You haven't seen the last of me!"
screeched Grizelda. She snapped her
fingers and vanished in a cloud of
stinking greeny-yellow sparks.

"Thanks for letting me stay," said
Nettle. "I'll watch over the Laughter Tree
if you like, and live here in the forest.
I was never very good at scaring people,

so maybe I can learn to make them laugh instead! Freya could come round sometimes and teach me some jokes."

The little dormouse clapped her paws. "I will!" she cried, happily. "And now you like laughing, there's something you have to do. Come with us to the Funny Fair!"

CHAPTER EIGHT

The Funny Fair!

"Ha ha!"

"Hee hee!"

Jess and Lily looked around at the Merry Meadow audience, grinning. All the animals were laughing at the show taking place on a little stage beneath the trees. Mr Cleverfeather had just finished

 91

demonstrating his Joke-o-Matic machine.
He had finally gathered enough laughter
to power it, and it was telling lots of very
silly knock-knock jokes.

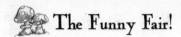

Next, Bella Tabbypaw the kitten ran on
stage with a bucket. "Shall I throw this
water over you?" she shouted.

"No!" shrieked the audience.

"I will!" said Bella, and everyone screeched with laughter. But it wasn't water at all! It was soft, sweet-scented petals. The animals laughed as the petals tumbled over them. Tallulah Slipperslide the otter had so many petals on her that she rolled onto her back, crying tears of laughter.

"This is the funniest show ever!" Lily giggled happily.

Goldie's green eyes gleamed. "It's thanks to you that everyone's happy again. Oh, look at the front row – the Twinkletail mice are wearing silly hats! Molly's is

a cupcake, and there's a banana, and a

canoe..."

"And the Flufftail
squirrels have made
funny masks!" Lily
said with a giggle.
"Sophie's got a
curly moustache!
And Woody's got

a unicorn horn! Isn't it lovely to see

the audience being just as silly as the

performers!"

The Paddlefoot beaver family came

onto the stage. "Micky the chicky did

a trick with a sticky," they sang. "His sticky got stucky and Micky got mucky." As they mixed up their words the whole family collapsed on the floor, giggling.

The audience roared with laughter!

"Freya's on next," said Jess. "I hope she doesn't get nervous again!"

A ball of golden-brown fur rolled onto the stage. As it came to a stop, it uncurled, and up jumped Freya, holding her handbag.

She grinned at the girls, then launched into her jokes. "Which side of a chicken has the most feathers?"

"We don't know!" the audience bellowed.

"The *out*side!" said Freya. "What's the Twinkletail mice's favourite game?"

"We don't know!" everyone called.

"Hide and *squeak*!" Freya said. "What do you wear when you go out in a storm?"

"We don't know!" everyone shouted.

"*Thunder*pants!" Freya laughed.

Finally, Freya said, "My new friend's

going to help me with my last joke."

Lily and Jess were thrilled when Nettle ran onto the stage and everyone cheered. She lifted Freya onto her hand, and the little dormouse began, "Nettle, did you hear what happened when Grizelda's spell went wrong and turned her nose upside down?"

Nettle shook her head. "No, what did happen when Grizelda's spell went wrong and turned her nose upside down?"

Freya grinned. "Every time she sneezed, her hat blew off!"

The crowd screamed with laughter.

Mr Longwhiskers could hardly get his breath, and the Prickleback hedgehogs giggled so much their prickles shook. The girls wiped away tears of laughter.

When the Funny Fair was over, all the performers came on stage to take a bow. Nettle was in the middle, beaming!

"It's nice to see Nettle happy," said Lily.

"But we must go home now, Goldie," said Jess. She went to the edge of the stage, and scooped Freya up for a hug.

Nettle stood nearby, looking shy, so Lily held out her arms.

The smiling witch ran to hug both girls.

"Thank you for making me laugh," she said, as the little dormouse jumped from Jess's hand onto Nettle's shoulder. "Freya and I will have lots of laughs together now we're friends."

"We will!" Freya said happily. "And thank you, girls, for helping me to stop

being nervous! Now I can tell jokes to all my friends!"

"You did an amazing job in the show, Freya!" said the girls. "Goodbye, everyone! Thanks for such a funny day!"

They followed Goldie through the sun-dappled forest. When they reached the Friendship Tree, Goldie said, "I'll come and visit you soon. After all, Grizelda's bound to be up to her tricks before long. We'll need your help."

The girls hugged her.

"We'll be ready," Jess promised.

"I know you will," said Goldie, happily.

She touched her paw to the tree's trunk and, instantly, a door appeared.

Jess opened it, and she and Lily stepped inside, into a shimmering golden glow. The forest faded and they felt the tingle that meant they were returning to their proper size.

As the light cleared, the girls stepped back into Brightley Meadow. They crossed the stream and, on the way back through Lily's garden, they passed the sad little fox cub.

"He's still not playing with the toys we made," said Jess. Then she felt something tickling her hand. "Hey! I forgot I'd tucked this in my belt!"

She pulled out the short, bent feather that Mr Fantail had given her. Then she used it to gently tickle the fox cub's nose.

He rolled onto his back, so she tickled his tummy. He batted the feather with his

paws, and she tickled him again.

"He's having fun at last!" said Lily. "I guess he really did just need the right toy to cheer him up — one with a little magic!"

Jess laughed. "If animals in our world could talk, I think that little fox cub would be giggling!"

The End

Lottie Littlestripe the badger has a problem –
none of the babies in the Fuzzy Nuzzle Nursery
can sleep! Could Grizelda have done something
to the Sweet Dreams Tree?

Find out in the next adventure,

Lottie Littlestripe's Midnight Plan

Turn over for a sneak peek . . .

The Sweet Dreams Tree had broad branches, with deep green leaves and large pink flowers. In the middle of the trunk was a hollow. Inside it, the tree's twinkling silver heart sat on a green mossy cushion. The girls knew that was the source of the tree's power.

"Those pink flowers are Dream Blossoms," whispered Goldie. "But there are usually lots more of them. Something is definitely wrong."

"They're beautiful," said Lottie. "They look soft and squashy, like candy floss!"

Jess gasped as a figure with a puffball

of yellow hair appeared from behind the trunk. "Dandelion!"

"Who is Dandelion?" asked Lottie, stretching up her stripy nose to see.

"She's one of the young witches that have been helping Grizelda," Goldie said. "I bet she's up to something bad."

Read

Lottie Littlestripe's Midnight Plan

to find out what happens next!

Puzzle Fun!

Can you match Freya Snufflenose
to the correct shadow?

A
B
C

Jess and Lily's Animal Facts

Lily and Jess love lots of different animals –
both in Friendship Forest
and in the real world.

Here are their top facts about

DORMICE

like Freya Snufflenose:

- Dormice are found in Europe and Asia. The kind of dormouse that lives in the UK is called the hazel dormouse.

- If you spot a dormouse, you are very lucky! Dormice are nocturnal, so they only come out at night, and they are also very rare.

- The dormouse is a very active type of mouse. Dormice don't normally go onto the ground, but usually climb through trees and bushes.

- Dormice hibernate, sleeping all winter and waking up when it's warm.

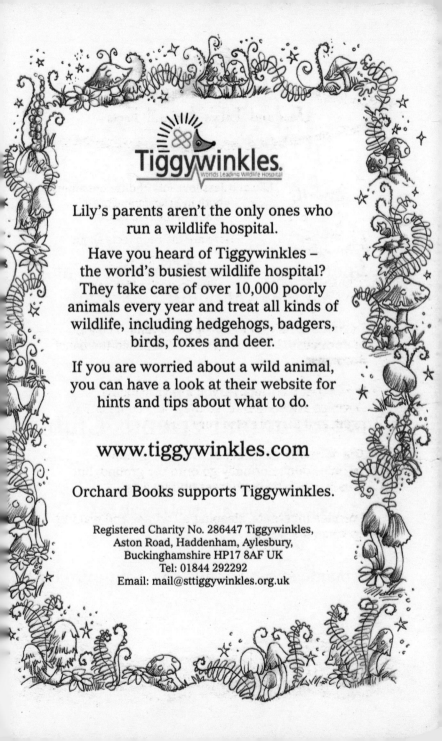

Tiggywinkles.
Worlds Leading Wildlife Hospital

Lily's parents aren't the only ones who run a wildlife hospital.

Have you heard of Tiggywinkles – the world's busiest wildlife hospital? They take care of over 10,000 poorly animals every year and treat all kinds of wildlife, including hedgehogs, badgers, birds, foxes and deer.

If you are worried about a wild animal, you can have a look at their website for hints and tips about what to do.

www.tiggywinkles.com

Orchard Books supports Tiggywinkles.

Registered Charity No. 286447 Tiggywinkles, Aston Road, Haddenham, Aylesbury, Buckinghamshire HP17 8AF UK
Tel: 01844 292292
Email: mail@sttiggywinkles.org.uk

Magic Animal Friends

Can you keep the secret?

There's lots of fun for everyone at
www.magicanimalfriends.com

Play games and explore the secret world of
Friendship Forest, where animals can talk!

Join the
Magic Animal Friends Club!

Special competitions

Exclusive content

All the latest Magic Animal Friends news!

To join the Club, simply go to

www.magicanimalfriends.com/join-our-club/